The Handkerchief Quilt

by **Carol Crane**
and illustrated by
Gary Palmer

To the family of Mrs. Anderson—
her five grandchildren, seven great-grandchildren,
and two great-great grandchildren.

—Carol

❀

In loving memory of my mother,
Doris Nell.

—Gary

Text Copyright © 2010 Carol Crane
Illustration Copyright © 2010 Gary Palmer

Sleeping Bear Press™

315 E. Eisenhower Parkway, Ste. 200
Ann Arbor, MI 48108
www.sleepingbearpress.com

© 2010 Sleeping Bear Press is an imprint of Gale,
a part of Cengage Learning.

Printed and bound in China.

First Edition

10 9 8 7 6 5 4 3 2 1

Library of Congress Cataloging-in-Publication Data

Crane, Carol, 1933-
The handkerchief quilt / written by Carol Crane; illustrated by Gary Palmer.
p. cm.
Summary: When a disastrous flood damages Parkland School, forcing it to close for
lengthy repairs, Miss Anderson, an elementary teacher, devises a way to raise money
to help buy replacement books.
ISBN 978-1-58536-344-5
[1. Teachers—Fiction. 2. Schools—Fiction. 3. Fund raising—Fiction. 4. Quilts—
Fiction.] I. Palmer, Gary, 1968- ill. II. Title.
PZ7.C8474Han 2010
[E]—dc22
2009036939

The town always started its day with the 7 a.m. factory whistle. Its long, shrill blasts hung as if suspended in air, and then, just for a moment, everything was quiet before the world of work started.

Children scrambled out of bed, mothers put breakfast on the table and packed lunches, and fathers started their work in the local automobile factory.

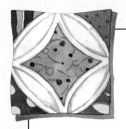
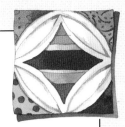

The sound of the whistle also started Miss Anderson's day. She taught at Parkland School; its old building sat on the only hill in town. For many years, Monday through Friday, with a basket swinging on her arm, she had walked to the same classroom. The schoolchildren were the spring in her steps, the beat of her heart.

Miss Anderson was a loving teacher. She always wore a long dress with two pockets and a belt. A handkerchief peeked out of each pocket; another was tucked in her belt and a fourth one always stuck out from the sleeve of her dress.

"You never know when a handkerchief might be needed for a nose, a cut, or a tear," she would say.

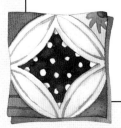
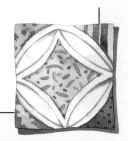

It was Thanksgiving week. Pictures of turkeys, Indians, and pilgrims had been drawn and colored, and then cut, pasted, and pinned to the corkboard, windows, and doors.

The week had passed quickly and on Wednesday afternoon the children went home to be with their families for the holiday. Everyone would return to school on Monday.

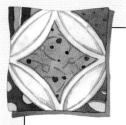
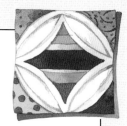

Miss Anderson lived in a small cottage with her cat, Eleanor. After her own quiet celebration, she gave a sigh and said to Eleanor, "I can do some reading, a little cleaning and, oh yes, decide what to do with my handkerchief collection. You may help me."

For years her students had given her handkerchiefs as gifts. Some of the treasured pieces of cloth came from faraway countries; others were made of material saved from worn-out aprons, dresses, or shirttails.

The handkerchiefs were first stored in a drawer, then in a large box, and finally, as the collection grew, moved to a cedar chest.

Miss Anderson opened the cedar chest. Eleanor was ready to help.

But as she sat and felt the different materials, admiring the designs and recalling the smiling face of a child handing her a handkerchief, Miss Anderson gave a little sigh. She repacked the chest and said to Eleanor, "There are too many good memories to part with."

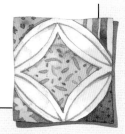

Over the holiday weekend the weather had turned bitterly cold. On Monday morning Miss Anderson, bundled in a long coat, boots, and a warm scarf wrapped around her neck, began her usual walk to school.

The path was slippery so she kept her eyes down and did not look up until she reached the steps of the school. A white layer of ice had formed under the heavy school door. She looked up at the windows; they were shimmering with frost.

She tried to open the door but it was stuck shut.

With a hard shove, Miss Anderson
opened the door. Stepping inside she
gasped in surprise. The hallway was a
slick skating pond and icicles hung from
the ceiling.

Mr. Post, the principal, yelled, "Stay out! The
furnace went out and the pipes burst. Water and
ice are everywhere!"

Parkland School was immediately closed.

Water from the second floor had poured down into the classrooms and the library. Books were swollen and heavy with water, their pages stuck together.

Mr. Post called an emergency meeting. It would be months before the school would be ready to reopen. New supplies, especially books, were needed, as well as a place to hold classes.

And there was little money with which to do it all.

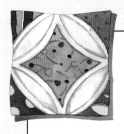
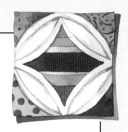

Thinking of her school in ruins, Miss Anderson tossed and turned in her bed that night. Eleanor, having lost her warm spot, jumped off the bed with a thud, startling her mistress.

A beam of moonlight coming through the bedroom window shone down on the handkerchief chest. Eleanor was sitting on top of the chest with a knowing look.

Miss Anderson smiled.

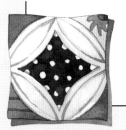

The next morning Miss Anderson found a sled in the garage. She carried box after box of handkerchiefs out to the sled.

Then, with a determined step, she pulled the sled to the fire station. Students' parents had been called to meet there.

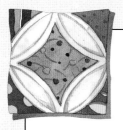

With a gentle voice, Miss Anderson spoke. "Each year my students have given me handkerchiefs as gifts. Using that fabric, along with any donations, I would like to ask each family to help make a handkerchief quilt. We could sell the quilt to raise money for books and supplies."

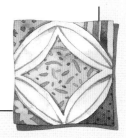

So for three weeks, families worked together, night and day, in shifts.

The men, fathers and grandfathers, used their design experience from the factory. And the women, mothers and grandmothers, applied their sewing skills.

Together they designed a pattern called "Cathedral Window."

The children, guided by Miss Anderson, took scissors and snipped and trimmed strips of cloth from all the handkerchiefs.

At last, with the strips of cloth laid out in a pattern, the women sat down with threaded needles and began to sew.

The soothing motion of needles going in and out set a rhythm for story-telling. Families, recognizing pieces of cloth, shared their history. Slowly, a beautiful quilt was born.

Now, thought Miss Anderson, I need to find it a proper home.

Finally, after several months, Parkland School reopened and the students were allowed to return.

The building was repaired but they still needed money for supplies and books.

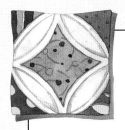
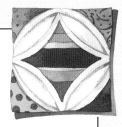

One day, not long after school had resumed, Miss Anderson received a letter. It was from a quilt museum in the East.

Children gathered around Miss Anderson as she opened up the envelope. It contained a letter, along with a check.

The handkerchief quilt was sold! There was enough money to buy books for the school library and paper for the students!

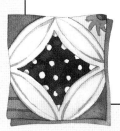
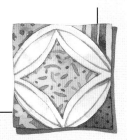

One morning in June after she arrived at school, Miss Anderson found her students and their parents waiting for her in her classroom.

A big red bow was tied to her reading rocker. They led her to her chair and presented her with a square flat box. As the parents clapped, the children wiggled with excitement while Miss Anderson opened the box.

Inside, wrapped in tissue paper, was a beautiful handkerchief, lovingly made from the remnants left from the quilt project and embroidered with the students' names.

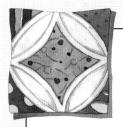
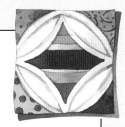

Author's Note

The fictional story you have just read is lovingly written in honor of and based on the life of my mother, Verna Elizabeth Oldenburg Anderson. She was an elementary school teacher for 30 years and opened her heart to parents and children alike.

In the 1940s and '50s, Flint, Michigan, was a bustling and vibrant community. Workers came from all over the country (and the world) to work in Flint's automobile factories, bringing their families with them.

Parkland School was a public school in Flint where my mother taught for a dozen years. She was known throughout the area as everyone's reading teacher. A two-story brick building, Parkland School sat on a high hill overlooking a baseball field and Berston Field House. The school opened in 1914 and closed in 1976; it has since been torn down.

The Handkerchief Quilt is based on an incident that occurred at Parkland in the early '50s when a disastrous water leak caused significant damage. My mother organized a quilting bee to help buy replacement books and supplies. To create the quilt her collection of handkerchiefs (gifts from schoolchildren over the years) was used, along with pieces of fabric such as shirttails, aprons, and dress hems donated by many families.

At the end of her career, my mother came down with Guillain-Barré syndrome. Her recovery was slow and to help improve dexterity in her fingers, she took up quilting again at the hospital. She did make another quilt, which I cherish.

I hope that you have enjoyed this personal story. And I express many thanks to the staff members at Sloan Museum and the Flint Public Library who helped in my research.

—Carol Crane

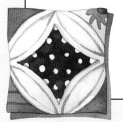